Quiz No 218254
The Curious Demise of a Contrary Cat

Berry, Lynne
B.L.: 1.9
Points: 0.5   LY

THE CURIOUS DEMISE OF A
CONTRARY CAT

QUIZ NO 218254

Bl 1.8

01142

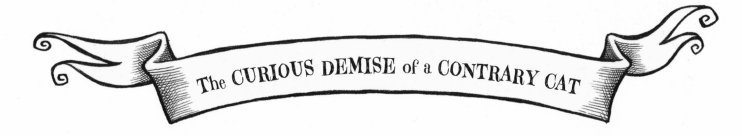

The CURIOUS DEMISE of a CONTRARY CAT

Story by Lynne Berry
Pictures by Luke LaMarca

SIMON AND SCHUSTER
London   New York   Toronto   Sydney

SIMON AND SCHUSTER

First published in Great Britain in 2006 by Simon & Schuster UK Ltd

Africa House, 64-78 Kingsway, London WC2B 6AH

This paperback edition first published in 2006

Originally published in 2006 by Simon and Schuster Books For Young Readers

an imprint of Simon & Schuster Children's Publishing Division, New York

A CIP catalogue record for this book is available from the British Library upon request

ISBN 1 416 91745 4

EAN 9781416917458

Printed in China

1 3 5 7 9 10 8 6 4 2

To John—L. B.
For Mom & Dad—L. L.

On a pale grey night with a bright full moon, Witch was dressing for a bash.

"Cat," said Witch, "fetch me a hat!"
But Cat was busy, chasing Rat.

"Cat?" said Witch.

"Purr?" said Cat.

"Hat!" said Witch.

"GRRRRR," said Cat.

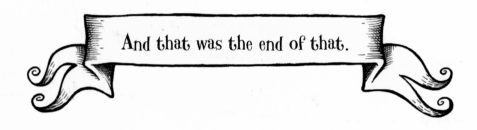

And that was the end of that.

Witch got her own hat. "DRAT THAT CAT!"

On a pale grey night with a bright full moon, Witch was greeting Ghost and Bat.

"Cat," said Witch, "fetch me a chair!"
But Cat was busy, eyeing Bat.

"Cat?" said Witch.

"Purr?" said Cat.

"Chair!" said Witch.

"GRRRRR," said Cat.

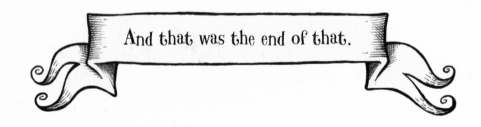

And that was the end of that.

Witch got her own chair. "DRAT THAT CAT!"

"But have a seat, dear Madame Ghost."

On a pale grey night with a bright full moon, Witch was serving punch and pie.

"Cat," said Witch, "fetch me a cup!"
But Cat was busy, stalking Ghost.

"Cat?" said Witch.

"Purr?" said Cat.

"CUP!" said Witch.

"GRRRRR," said Cat.

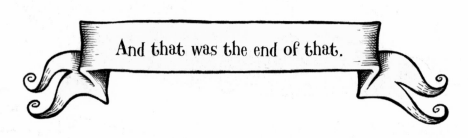

And that was the end of that.

Witch got her own cup. "DRAT THAT CAT!"

"Some putrid punch, dear Mr Troll?"

On a pale grey night with a bright full moon, Witch was wishing for a jig.

"Cat," said Witch, "fetch me a fife!"
But Cat was busy, chasing Troll.

"Cat?" said Witch.

"Purr?" said Cat.

"FIFE!" said Witch.

"GRRRRR," said Cat.

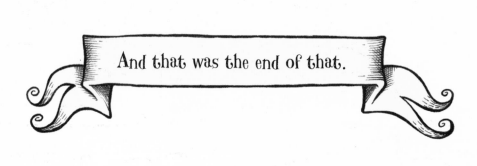

And that was the end of that.

Witch got her own fife. "DRAT THAT CAT!"

"But shall we dance, my Spooks and Sprites?"

On a pale grey night with a bright full moon, Witch was bidding guests goodbye.

"Cat," said Witch, "fetch me a cloak!"
But Cat was busy, spooking Sprite.

"Cat?" said Witch.

"Purr?" said Cat.

"CLOAK!" said Witch.

"GRRRRR," said Cat.

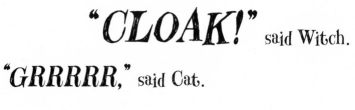

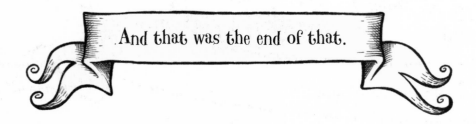

And that was the end of that.

Witch got her own cloak. "DRAT THAT CAT!"

"But let me see you out, dear Gnomes."

On a pale grey night with a bright full moon, Witch was cleaning cups and crumbs.

"Cat," said Witch, "fetch me a broom!"
But Cat was back to chasing Rat.

"Cat?" said Witch.

"Purr?" said Cat.

"BROOM!" said Witch.

"GRRRRR," said Cat.

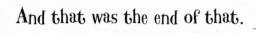
And that was the end of that.

Witch got her own broom. "DRAT THAT CAT!"

On a pale grey night with a bright full moon, Witch was brewing one last spell.

"Cat," said Witch, "fetch me a toad!"
But Cat was snoozing on the mat.

"Cat?" said Witch.

"Purr?" said Cat.

"*TOAD!!!*" cried Witch.

"*GRRR—
—rribbit?*"

And **THAT** was the end of Cat.

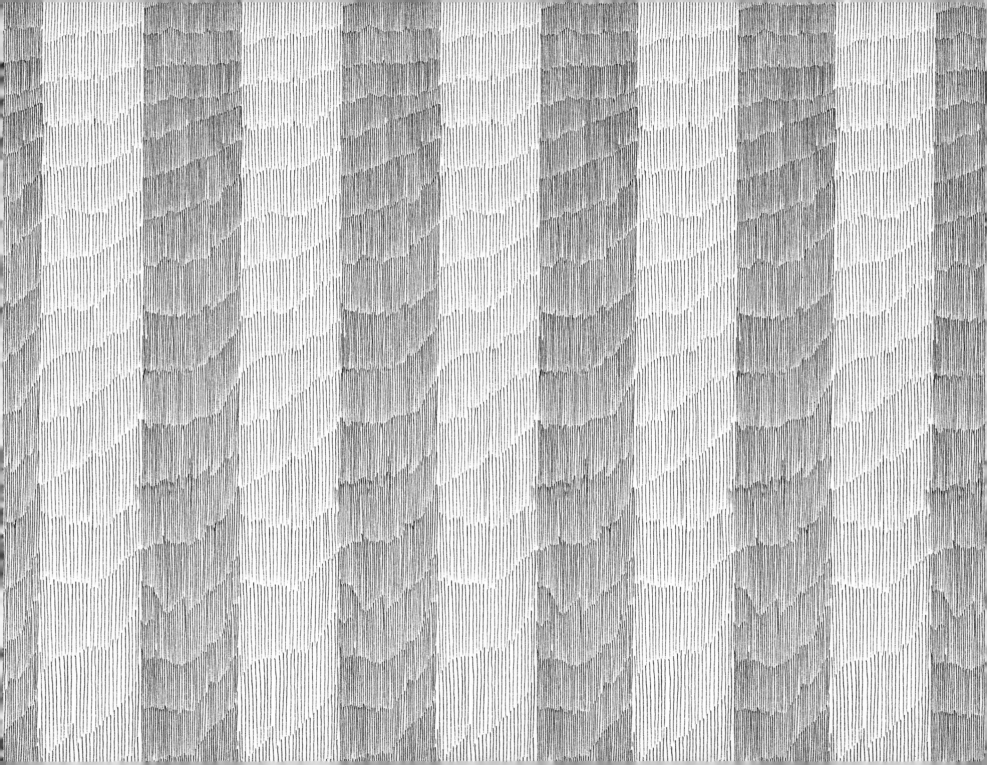